A Heroine's Journey

Order this book online at www.trafford.com
or email orders@trafford.com

Most Trafford titles are also available at major online book retailers.

Print information available on the last page.

ISBN: 978-1-6987-0465-4 (sc)
ISBN: 978-1-6987-0466-1 (e)

Illustrated by Pamela J Peck
Edited by Ken Johnson, MJ
Cover design/Artwork by Pamela J Peck
Layout and design by PJenesis Press

Trafford rev. 01/12/2021

Trafford
PUBLISHING®   www.trafford.com
North America & international
toll-free: 844-688-6899 (USA & Canada)
fax: 812 355 4082

A Heroine's Journey

A Viking Myth of Self-Discovery

Pamela J Peck, PhD

BY THE SAME AUTHOR

Morning Star

The Eucharist

LOST AND FOUND

The Cannibal's Cookbook

Tales from Cannibal Isle

COMING OF AGE IN ANTHROPOLOGY

A HERO'S JOURNEY

ALSO
ISLAND IN SPACE
(Editor and Co-author)

To the enduring contribution
of feminine energy to humankind

About the Narratives

This modern mythology was originally written by the author as part of a Lecture Series for a trans-Atlantic crossing from London to Boston on Royal Caribbean's beautiful cruise ship *Splendour of the Seas* in September of 1999.

Penned by the author "The Vinland Narratives", their purpose is twofold; first, to share history and culture of the geographical areas travelled during the ship's itinerary and, secondly, to lay the groundwork for a much deeper purpose: illumination of anthropologist Joseph Campbell's teachings about the mythological Hero's Journey.

The Vinland Narratives

THE COMMENTARY

The Vinland Narratives were offered to cruise
passengers on days when the *Splendour of the Seas*
was "At Sea" as here recorded.

In this printed version of the Talks, an introductory
Prologue sets the stage for the Narratives,
 each of which is followed by a brief Commentary.

A summary of the stages in the classic Hero's Journey
is provided at the conclusion of the Narratives.

THE ITINERARY

Day 0	London
Day 1	At Sea
Day 2	Bergen, Norway
Day 3	Shetland Islands
Day 4	Faroe Islands
Day 5	At Sea
Day 6	Akureyri, Iceland
Day 7	Reykjavik, Iceland
Day 8	At Sea
Day 9	At Sea
Day 10	At Sea
Day 11	St. John's, Newfoundland
Day 12	At Sea
Day 13	Bar Harbour, Maine
Day 14	Boston, Massachusetts

In the Autumn of the Year
One Thousand, Nine Hundred
And Ninety-nine

The Vinland Narratives

Prologue

Imagine if you will, a land with a Viking name, endowed with Viking history, yet laying an ocean away from the shores of Scandinavia. And imagine that in this place, far beyond the islands of ice and snow that emerge out of the sea mists of the North Atlantic Ocean, warm breezes deposit sweet-tasting dew on the summer grasses, and long days of sunlight permit wild grape vines to blossom and grow. Here, further west than any Europeans have ever sailed before, the Vikings, they say, came to this favoured place and gave to it the name of Vinland.

Imagine now a boy, who grows up on the coast of Norway. The boy has heard the stories of greatness about his cultural past. How, as far back as a thousand years or more, Scandinavian people sailed across the North Atlantic in small, open ships and discovered a New World. It was not Columbus, he learned, who first arrived in America from Europe; it was his own people, the Norsemen, known as Vikings. Further than Iceland, further than Greenland, or Baffin Island or even Newfoundland they sailed.... Down, down the east coast of what is now the continent of North America. And somewhere on that coastline, they stepped ashore and founded the fabled land of wild grapes and sweet-tasting dew.

But history could not—or would not—verify the fact. Almost a thousand years later, Vinland remains an unsolved mystery. Is there such a place? If so, did the Vikings really manage to settle there? No authoritative body will say yes to either query. And until someone can prove the fact, the Scandinavians will not be properly credited with discovering the New World.

When the boy grew to be a man, he determined to go in search of the missing land. He scoured every piece of local legend for evidence, then, following the faint and mysterious clues, set out in a small open ship, replicating an ancient Viking voyage to the New World. He sailed from Norway to the Shetland Islands, then to the Faroe Islands, across to Iceland and down the North American coastline past Newfoundland.

Heroic indeed, but as it turned out, the hero of a fated journey. For when the man returned to his native Norway the following year, confident he had found the fabled land— but lacking the evidence to prove it—he became the laughingstock of those who considered Vinland nothing more than a piece of fanciful Viking mythology. To the end, the man was true to his quest, and he departed from the world, still convinced that the evidence was there to be uncovered, somewhere in what is now the state of Massachusetts.

Imagine now a girl, a daughter of this fated wanderer, who grows up in her father's shadow. The memory of the past has created in her a gnawing restlessness and overshadowed any goals she might have had for herself. It has driven her to reinvent herself in the image of her father in an attempt to uncover the illusive proof that would restore his reputation.

Imagine it is early autumn in the final year before a new millennium. More than a thousand years have passed since the Norsemen first sailed toward the Americas in their small, open boats. And now, a beautiful ship arrives at the port in Bergen, Norway as it traces the route of the Vikings along a chain of islands separating the Old World from the New.

Bergen, with its rugged glacial scenery, ancient stone churches, verdant gardens and sparkling fjords. The picturesque land that inspired the Norwegian composer Edward Grieg to create his lyrical music....

The girl bids farewell to her mother and boards the elegant ship. She earns passage as a hostess in the disco bar on the eleventh deck, fittingly called the Viking Crown Lounge. In two weeks, the ship will dock in Boston. The girl believes this is the place where she will find the missing piece of the puzzle to restore her father's good name. For Boston is the most likely place the Vikings would have stepped ashore in the land known as Massachusetts.

And a heroine's journey begins . . .

COMMENTARY ON THE PROLOGUE

What is the heroine's journey? It is a journey whereby the heroine leaves the familiar ordinary world and ventures into the unknown in order to return with a new insight. It is the road less traveled. There are dangers along the way, and while many myths portray these dangers as physical, they are more properly psychological ones. For the heroine must make a shift from trying to change the world to changing her mind about the world. The alternative is to settle for the beliefs, the rituals and the conditioned social behavior of the particular culture into which she had been born and raised. In short, it is to live the unexamined life.

The heroine's journey is the stuff of classical mythology. In the course of the Vinland Narratives, we along with our heroine will hear classical myths that represent different cultures, are recorded in different languages, and appear in different centuries spanning more than 3000 years. Yet they all tell the same story.

Not on the surface. On the surface they appear at the textual level to be very different. But when we look beneath the text, to the subtext, we see they have a similar structure. And when we go even deeper, from the subtext to the context, we discover they all carry the same message. That is the power and the purpose of mythology. To paraphrase Joseph Campbell, mythology is the secret opening through which the eternal energy of the cosmos pours into human culture. It has always been the prime function of mythology, states Campbell, to supply the symbols to carry the human spirit forward. The symbols of mythology are not manufactured, and they cannot be invented or suppressed. They are the spontaneous outpourings of the human psyche. That is why all the stories bear the same message.

The Vinland Narratives is a modern Hero's Journey. The hero, of course, might be male or female. In either case, the hero(ine) is the main character in the story just as each of us is the main character in our own story. The question is this: Is our story an heroic one? For heroes and heroines are in short supply because few of us venture into the unknown. For the most part, we stay within the safe confines of what we take to be the tried and true. So the purpose of the mythological hero's journey is to discover the hero(ine) within ourselves.

Narrative I

On the Viking Trail

Search for a Missing Land

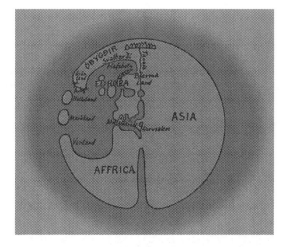

Imagine if you will, the *Splendour of the Seas* leaving its moorings on the southwesterly tip of Norway. It plies the open water of the sea of islands bearing Scandinavian names. Night falls. There is silence apart from the gentle splashing of waves against the ship's prow. Most of the passengers are asleep. But not the girl. She stands at her post in the Viking Crown Lounge. And when all the late-night "party animals" have been served their cocktails and beer and wine, she pauses and looks out into the black, star-lit sky.

The girl knows some things about Viking history. But why, she wonders, after so many years and so many searches could Vinland remain an unsolved mystery. After all, there are the sagas and the runic stones attesting to the presence of Vikings in the New World. But there is no conclusive evidence about Vinland. What is so elusive about this place!

Now, as fate— or destiny— would have it, there is a very colorful character on board this beautiful ship. He is a harbour pilot, hailing from the Canadian island of Newfoundland, returning home after a sojourn in the British Isles. Having spent the better part of a lifetime guiding ships in and out of the rocky port of St. John's, he never grew accustomed to—nor, to be honest, comfortable with—the speed of air travel, preferring to stand on his own two sea legs across the North Atlantic instead. Before retiring for the evening, he heads to the Viking Crown Lounge for a nightcap of his customary drink.

"I'll have a screech," he says to the Norwegian girl.

"A screech, sir?"

"Ah, you're new on the ship, eh?" he says.

"Yes, sir."

"Well, screech is a Newfie drink. It's rum. But not just any rum. It's the dregs from the bo'um of the barrel."

"From the bo'um?" she says.

"You don't know what a bo'um is? There's the top and there's the bo'um.

"Oh, you mean the bottom."

"Yeah, the bo'um."

"Right, sir, I'll see if we have some."

She takes the order to the bar tender. "Screech!" he says to her. "For a Newfie, right? They're a different lot. I think their taste buds are numbed from eating too many cod tongues. Tell him we don't have screech, but we do have rum."

The girl delivers the message.

"Right, then," the Newfoundlander says, "bring me a bo'ole of rum."

"A bo'ole, sir?"

"You know, what the rum comes in. A bo'ole."

"Oh, you mean a bottle."

"Yeah, a bo'ole."

"Right, sir."

The girl returns with the bottle of rum—and a glass. "You shouldn't drink too much of that at one time," she says. "It will dehydrate your body."

"It will, eh!" The Newfie digs into his pocket and pulls out that little blue stateroom charge card. "So, how long is your contract?" he asks the girl.

"Oh, no contract, sir. I am on my way to Boston."

"Boston. And what is your business there?"

"I am searching for Vinland."

"Vinland. Well, if you want to find Vinland, you need not sail all the way to Boston. Vinland is in m' own back yard."

"In your back yard, sir?"

"Newfoundland."

"Oh no, sir" she replies instantly, "Vinland is not in Newfoundland. It is somewhere in Massachusetts."

"Oh, I don't think so," he replies. "It's in L'anse aux Meadows, on the northern tip of Newfoundland. There's lots of evidence the Vikings were there."

"But that's not Vinland," she says, "Grapes do not grow in Newfoundland."

"Well, it's not likely there were grapes growin' anywhere the Vikings landed," he responds. "They probably said that to make people want to go there. Just like they gave that big sheet of ice the name of Greenland to entice people to go and settle there."

13

"No," she says. "I know that Vinland is somewhere in Massachusetts. My father said so."

"Your father. That's interestin', eh. Two people in the same family with the same callin'. It's very unusual."

"Oh, it's not my calling. I just need to clear his name."

"For what purpose, dare I ask?"

"So they will stop laughing about him."

"Well, laughter is good. People laugh about Newfies all the time. So you know what we do? We laugh at ourselves. Let people laugh. Keeps 'em young an' healthy."

"Well, I know about keeping young and healthy. And it doesn't come from laughing at people."

"It doesn't, eh. What does it come from then?"

"Oh, it's an old Scandinavian secret."

"A secret, eh?" he says.

"Well, not really," she responds, "because everybody knows it."

"Well, maybe everybody knows it where you come from. But there are a lot of people where you're goin' who have spent a lot of time and money searchin' for the fountain of youth."

"Yeah, well, I have to do right by my father."

The Newfoundlander pauses. "If you want to do right by your father," he states, "you can best do it by livin' your life rather than tryin' to relive his."

The girl does not respond.

The old seaman notices the girl is wearing a pendant that hangs from a chain around her neck. It's a carving in stone that looks like the letter L in an upside down and slightly sideways position.

"That's an interestin' necklace," he says, "What does it mean?"

"Oh, that's a runestone," she replies.

"A runestone? What's that?"

"Well, the runes are an old Nordic alphabet that was first used for magical purposes."

"Magical, eh!" he says.

"Yes. The runes are linked with the Norse god Odin, who gained the wisdom of the runes by hanging on the 'tree of life' for nine days and nights. According to the Legend, 24 runes, known as the Elfer or Common Futhark, were revealed to Odin and are the basis of the Poetic Edda, which consists of 39 poems."

"Hold on a minute," he interjects, "I thought you said it was an alphabet."

"Yes," she replies, "it is, but each of the 24 runes has a verse that relates to it. Like the first rune, for example. It looks a bit like the letter F, and it's called Fehu. Here's the verse that goes with it:

Wealth is a comfort to everyone,
Yet each must give freely,
If he will glory in heaven.

"You see, Fehu means 'cattle', and back then owning cattle was the measure of wealth and prosperity. So the rune represents plenty, but also cautions that wealth must be shared with others."

"That's very interestin'," he says.

"Yes. All 24 runes have a verse like that and each one has a kind of spiritual code locked inside it."

"And what is your rune?" he asks

"Well, it's called the Laguz, the L-rune," she says.

"What does it mean?"

"Well, the L-rune is the symbol for water."

"Ah, and why did you choose that symbol?"

"Oh, no, people don't just choose a rune," she says. "When you have a decision to make or need direction, you concentrate on that and then you reach into the bag of runes and, without looking, take one."

"Ah, and why do you think you picked the symbol of water?" he asks.

"I don't know. Because of my father, I guess."

"Oh, did he pick the same rune?" the seaman asks.

"No, his was Sowulo, the S-rune. It's a symbol for the sun as a guiding light to seafarers.

Sun to the seafarer,
Is always confidence',
When they move across
The fishers' bath,
'Til the sea-horse
Brings them to land.'

"Hmmm. And what does the poem for the L-rune say?" he wants to know.

"It says," the girl responds...

Water to land-folk
Seems tedious,
If they venture forth
In an unstable boat.
The sea waves will foam
And the sea horse
Heeds not the bridle.

"That's interestin', eh," he says. And what does it mean to you?"

"I guess that I should take a more stable boat than my father did," she replies. "That's why I'm crossing the North Atlantic on a cruise ship."

He laughs. "To search fer Vinland, eh?"

"Yes," she replies.

"And how will you know it when you get there?" he says.

"I'll look for the runestone. You know, the big stone carvings that the Vikings left as markers wherever they went. My father is sure it is there, somewhere in the land of Massachusetts."

"And the runestone would confirm it is Vinland, right?"

"Yes, of course," she says.

The harbour pilot grows silent, and then he speaks. "Imagine," he says, "you are given a choice between discoverin' two things. The first is a new idea revealed to you as a story. The second is a new event, revealed to you as history. Which would you choose?"

"Oh, I would choose history," she replies without hesitation, "because I am only interested in the truth."

"Okay, if you are serious about findin' the truth," he says, "there is somethin' I want you to do when we get to Iceland. Go to the library in Reykjavik and read there what they say about the Icelandic sagas, especially about the Eric Saga and the Saga of the Greenlanders."

"Oh, I already know Viking history," replies the girl. "I just want to find the runestone."

"Well, tell you what," he says, "Just take another look at 'em. And when you're done doin' that, find out what they say about the runestones."

"Viking runes and Viking sagas, right?" the girl asks.

"Viking runes and Viking sagas," he repeats. He downs what remains of a single glass of rum, points to the bottle, indicating for her to put it aside for him—and then he bids the Norwegian girl goodnight.

COMMENTARY ON NARRATIVE I

The first three of twelve steps of the Hero's Journey have now happened. We begin in . . .

1. THE ORDINARY WORLD

Something takes our hero(ine) from the ordinary mundane world into a special world, new and alien. S/he is like "a fish out of water". What is our heroine's ordinary world? She is a young girl growing up in the Norwegian city of Bergen. Nothing uproots her in a purely physical sense; she personally identifies with an issue that culminates in . . .

2. A CALL TO ADVENTURE

A challenge, something that makes leaving the ordinary world an imperative. In this case, it is a psychological problem: people are laughing about her father's unproved claims to discovering a Viking settlement in the new world. She feels a need to prove him right to clear his name. Her action leads to . . .

3. MEETING OF THE MENTOR

Usually a wise old man or woman which is symbolic of the parent/child or teacher/student relationship. In Star Wars, it is Obi Ben Kenobi. In Mary Tylor Moore's world, it is Lou Grant. In this case, a harbour pilot from Newfoundland. The function of the mentor is to help the heroine face the unknown. But the mentor can go only so far. Eventually, the heroine must face the unknown alone. Now we are ready for the long journey at sea. Every myth has a long and perilous journey. Not perilous in the physical sense for it is a psychological challenge. The physical journey is a metaphor.

Narrative II

Viking Runes, Viking Sagas

Tracking an Unsolved Mystery

𝕴𝖒𝖆𝖌𝖎𝖓𝖊 𝖎𝖋 𝖞𝖔𝖚 𝖜𝖎𝖑𝖑, the *Splendour of the Seas* pulling away from its berth in Reykjavik and heading into the open sea. Imagine the passengers resting their feet after a glorious day on the banks of Kerid, that green lake formed more than 3000 years ago at the bottom of a volcanic crater. Night falls; the passengers enjoy their dinners, take in the entertainment and make their way to their staterooms. The winds are calm; the sea is mild. (Okay, the winds are howling, and the sea is rough.)

Imagine now the Newfoundland harbour pilot makes his way to the Viking Crown Lounge for his customary nightcap of rum. He knows the Norwegian girl will return to the ship with some unsettling information. He is not surprised to see her once again standing there, staring into the sky.

"Did you read about the Icelandic sagas?" he asks when she returns with an empty glass and his bottle of rum.

"Yes," comes the reserved reply.

"And?"

"They say there's no truth in it. That it's just pagan mythology about legendary heroes."

"Ah, yes," he responds, "and that is why it is a significant contribution to Icelandic literature. Heroism is praised, and while much is said of fate, the characters seem to control their own destinies."

"But they say it's not true. And that it's full of paradox."

"Yes, quite right. That makes it more excellent still," he says.

"I don't think you heard me," she replies. "They are saying it's just a mediaeval story."

"Ah, yes, I almost forgot, you are only interested in history, right."

"Right."

"And did you find history?"

"Yes. The Eric Saga and the Saga of the Greenlanders are histories," she replies.

"Okay. What do they say about your Vikings?"

"They confirm that the first Europeans to reach America came by way of Iceland and Greenland," she says. "The next wave of Europeans, like Columbus, Cabot and Champlain, didn't arrive until five hundred years later. Unlike them, the Vikings were not interested in international trade, and governments did not sponsor them. They were just family men, farmers and hunters and fishermen, looking for new homes, and their movement across the North Atlantic took more than a century."

"And where do they say these Vikings went?" he asks her.

"They say they explored the North American coast northwards to the Arctic and probably southwards to New England. They say they didn't go up the St. Lawrence River or venture inside the continent. But that can't be true because of Viking runestones found in Oklahoma and Minnesota."

"Ah, the runestones," he says, "we'll come back to that. What about Eric the Red and his son Leif the Lucky? What did you read about them?"

"It said little is known about Eric's early years. They don't even know if he was born in Norway. They think maybe he was born in Iceland."

"And what else?" the harbour pilot asks.

"In 982 he killed a man in Iceland," she says, "and he was outlawed for three years. He spent them exploring the west coast of Greenland. He returned to Iceland to organize a colonizing company to occupy the new country to which he gave the enticing name 'Greenland' just like you said, in order to attract settlers. Then in 986 he led a flotilla of twenty-five ships, and fourteen of them made it to Greenland."

"That's all?" asks the harbour pilot.

"No. In the same year an Icelandic merchant sailed from Iceland to spend Christmas with his father, who had immigrated to Greenland with Eric. The merchant was driven far off course in storms and fog. When the weather cleared, he and his traveling companions saw land that was wooded and dotted with small hills. They sailed north and came to a flat, forested land and then to a mountainous coast with glaciers. They did not put ashore at any of the three lands sighted. These places were most likely Newfoundland, Labrador and Baffin Island."

"But no Vinland, eh. So what happened after that?"

"Well," she replies, "people don't agree on what happened after that. But it is certain that Leif the Lucky did land either by accident or by design on the American mainland about the year 1000 and that the southernmost part of the coast he visited received the name 'Vinland'."

"You're certain of that, eh?"

"Yes. And in the next two decades, a small number of expeditions visited the mainland, and attempted to found a colony. It was abandoned after two or three years—but not before the first European child had been born in America. They named him Snorri. This expedition took place somewhere between 1003 and 1014. I say this was in Massachusetts. I just need to find the runestone to prove it."

"Well, you see," responds the harbour pilot, "the problem is this. These early voyages and settlements of the Vikings have resulted in sagas with different and contradictory interpretations. Not only that, the sagas and the runestones cannot be verified by archaeological evidence."

"That's not true," challenges the girl.

"Well, the two most important historical sources are the Eric Saga and the Saga of the Greenlanders. And they are supposed to describe the same events: the settlement of Greenland and the voyages from there to various parts of the east coast of North America. But people can't agree which is the more authentic and reliable report. Not only that, it seems that the Saga of the Greenlanders was composed before 1200 and the Eric Saga almost five hundred years later. Now that's a very long time after these events were supposed to have taken place. And there is not much archaeological evidence about visits or settlements of the Vikings south of the Gulf of St. Lawrence. What has been done has yielded no results, except for the excavations of your own countryman, Helge Ingstad in L'ans aux Meadows, Newfoundland."

"But according to both of those Sagas," the girl protests, "the Vinland that Leif the Lucky discovered and wintered in about the year 1000 had wild grape vines."

"Maybe it was maple or birch alder," suggests the old seaman.

"But there was also dew on the grass that was very sweet," she says. "And the cattle could forage for themselves in winter because there was no frost and the grass barely withered. And what about this? Day and night were of more equal length than in Iceland and about the time of the winter solstice the sun rose about 9:00 a.m. and set about 3:30 pm. And when Leif returned to Greenland, he brought a cargo of grapes and timber."

"But nothin' in what you've just said has enabled anyone to locate Vinland," he replies.

29

"Except to conclude," she counters, "that it must be a place where grapes grow, and the winters are mild. In working out the location, some people have placed Vinland as far south as Florida."

"And some as far north as Labrador," comes the old seaman's response.

"I say it's in Massachusetts," she states, "and I am going to find the runestone to prove it! The Eric Saga gives the sailing directions and describes the places they visited. It has to be there."

"Well," he cautions her, "people have been searchin' ever since 1837. One scholar thinks that Helluland and Markland are real, but that Vinland is a wholly mythical place."

"No way!" exclaims the girl.

"Well, if we are to believe those Sagas at all," he says, "here's what I think. Helluland must be Baffin Island and Markland must be some part of Labrador or possibly Newfoundland. And Vinland, well, the most plausible region answerin' the general description is, as you say, some part of New England. But not a single relic of Vinland has ever been found there while Viking traces have been discovered in Newfoundland. So I say Vinland is in Newfoundland."

"No, it can't be," comes her defiant reply.

"Well, Helge Ingstad found seven houses near L'Anse aux Meadows in northern Newfoundland in 1961, datin' from the eleventh century. One of the houses was twenty meters long, divided into five rooms that you could enter from a passageway that ran the whole length of the house. This type of construction, accordin' to Ingstad, was common in Norway around 1000."

"They were Norse houses," states the girl, "but they weren't Leif's houses or Vinland houses."

"Unless you accept Ingstad's contention," he replies, "that there were two Vinlands, a northern one and a southern one. 'Vinland' may even have been used to designate all the territories visited by Icelanders south of Markland."

"No," she says, "the location of Leif's Vinland must have just been forgotten."

"Well," he responds, "you would need proof, somethin' to verify that the Vikings actually ventured on the North American mainland."

"Well, they did, and there is proof!" she responds. "You're forgetting about the runestones."

"What about them?" he challenges.

"The Heavener Runestone. On Poteau Mountain in Oklahoma. It's a slab of stone 12 feet tall, 10 feet wide, and 16 inches thick, like a billboard. And there's writing on it. Eight letters from the runic alphabet.

"A number of people in the 1800's saw the stone and named it 'Indian Rock', although the Indians had no alphabet. In the 1830's some native people saw the writing but couldn't read it. In 1923 the lettering was submitted to the Smithsonian Institute and it was identified as letters of the Norse runes, and they figured out the markings represent the date November 11, 1012. The stone must have been made by ancient Vikings because they found two more runestones nearby, another smaller inscription of eight runes at the foothill of Poteau Mountain 14 miles away, and another stone with five runes in another part of Oklahoma."

"And what do you conclude from this?" he asks.

"But wait, there's more," she says. "In 1986, it was found that these five runestones had apparently been made even two or three centuries earlier, before the year 800. They made translations in words, not numbers, and found out the second and eighth runes are actually the letter L,—the same as my runestone—which permitted them to say that the Heavener runes are G-L-O-M-E-D-A-L, meaning Glome's Valley, which is a land claim. The other Poteau runes that are similar are a memorial to the same man. They read, 'Magic or protection to Gloie.' That was his nickname. The other runestone is the name 'Medok', and it was probably a gravestone. Two more runestones near Poteau Mountain don't have enough runes for a translation, but the four stones were placed in a straight line, miles apart. And the inscriptions are all from the oldest 24-rune alphabet, used from 300 until 800 in Scandinavia."

"So what is your theory about them?" he asks the girl.

"Well," she replies, "my father thought Norse explorers crossed the Atlantic, rounded the tip of Florida into the Gulf of Mexico and sailed up the Mississippi River. And because of the grammar used on the Poteau Runestone, they must have also traveled up the Arkansas and Poteau Rivers somewhere around the year 750."

"But nobody believes these runestones were put there by Vikings", he says. "It's the same with the Kensington Stone. It has been controversial ever since it was discovered in 1898. Some say it was a hoax."

"Then why do the people of Kensington have a big monument to it?" she challenges.

"Well, why do they also have a statue of Christopher Columbus in the same town?" he replies.

"No. This proves the Vikings discovered America many centuries before Columbus."

"Well, to my way of thinkin'," replies the harbour pilot, "the runestones are like the sagas. They are more story than history".

"Well," she says, "I can't imagine a bunch of illiterate farmers from Oklahoma or Minnesota carving a language they had never seen in a slab of rock just to start a story. Viking runes and Viking sagas are not stories, they are histories."

The Newfoundlander pauses, then he speaks. "The distinction you make between story and history is a very tenuous one," he says. "You are lookin' for truth only in history—and there may well be more truth in story."

33

"How can there be truth in a story?" challenges the girl.

"Ah, that," he replies as he empties his glass of rum, "I will tell you tomorrow."

COMMENTARY ON NARRATIVE II

PATH OF THE HERO'S JOURNEY

1. The Ordinary World
2. The Call to Adventure
3. Meeting of the Mentor

And now we come to . . .

4. REFUSAL OF THE CALL

This one is about fear. The heroine expresses reluctance — because she is facing the greatest of all fears — fear of the unknown. She is not yet fully committed to the challenge and may be thinking of turning back. Something else needs to happen to get the heroine past this point. For example, in Star Wars, Luke refuses Obi Wan's call, then returns to his farmhouse to find it has been destroyed. In our case, the heroine refuses the explanation offered by the mentor. She is not prepared to rethink her quest. She also questions the harbour pilot's notion that there can be truth in a story.

Narrative III
Ancient Rhymes, Ancient Mariners

The Path of the Hero's Journey

Imagine if you will, the *Splendour of the Seas* plying the open waters between Iceland and Newfoundland. It is a marginal space and a marginal time. They have left behind the last island that belongs to the great continent of Europe. Ahead is the first one on their voyage that claims affinity with the continent of North America. It is a passage between the Old World and the New.

Darkness of night reveals a panorama of stars. The girl gazes at the heavenly scene through the windows of the Viking Crown Lounge as she looks forward to another conversation with the harbour pilot. She cannot help but feel a twinge of excitement tonight, as though she also is moving from something old to something new. She cannot put her finger on it, but it seems to have something to do with what the old seaman had said about there being as much truth in story as in history. Somehow, although it makes no sense to her right now, she has the feeling it also has something to do with leading her to her goal.

The harbour pilot enters and discovers the girl once again staring into the sky.

"Tell me", he says, "what do you see?"

"Stars", she replies, as she places his partially filled bottle of rum on the table.

"Anythin' else?" he asks.

"No, just stars in a black sky."

"I see a story," he states.

"A story?"

"Yes, a story."

The girl looks at him curiously. "I don't see any story."

"It all depends on the way you look at it," he replies, as he pours the rum into a glass. "You have to see with your imagination. Like the ancient Egyptians. They divided the brighter stars into groups. Later the Greeks did the same thing. And maybe they had a better imagination because these are the groups we still use today."

The harbour pilot points out the window.

"The most familiar one here in the northern sky is Ursa Major—the Great Bear of mythology. It's autumn now, so Ursa Major is low on the horizon. Some people know it as the Big Dipper because those seven bright stars form the shape of a saucepan. Now, the two stars opposite the handle point to Polaris, the North Star. That star is always north. If we were at the North Pole, it would be directly overhead. Now let your eye follow down to those stars that look like a "w". That's Cassiopeia. Above Cassiopeia, that cluster is Cepheus. Next, look across from Cassiopeia to the first bright cluster; that's Andromeda. At a point below and between these two last clusters is one called Perseus. You can see this constellation better in winter because that's when all the stars are above the horizon.

"Now, there is a great story about these stars.

"In Greek mythology, the great god Zeus comes to a woman and makes her the mother of Perseus. But the woman's father learns from the oracle of Delphi that his daughter will have a son who will grow up to kill his grandfather, which is himself. So the man locks his daughter and Perseus into a chest and throws the chest into the sea.

"Perseus and his mother—inside the chest—wash up on the shore of a kingdom. The king there falls in love with the woman but doesn't want her son around. So the king tricks the young Perseus into goin' on a dangerous mission to the extremities of the earth where there are dreaded monsters and sea serpents. After a very long time and many difficult encounters, Perseus finally achieves the impossible mission.

"On his way back home, Perseus reaches the kingdom of Ethiopia and finds the country in a state of desolation. Cassiopeia, wife of King Cepheus of Ethiopia, upsets the sea god Neptune by boastin' that she is more beautiful than the sea-nymphs. Neptune gets angry and sends a very mean monster to terrorize the kingdom. In their terror, the Ethiopians appeal to their god in the desert who explains that Neptune will be appeased only if Cepheus will sacrifice his daughter Andromeda to the monster. Sadly, the king agrees, and Andromeda is chained to a rock.

"Now the hero Perseus comes along. He finds unhappy Andromeda chained to the rock, awaitin' death—and he falls in love with her at first sight. With great difficulty, he kills the monster, saves Andromeda and marries her. Perseus then takes Andromeda back to the place where he has left his mother with the jealous king, only to find that his mother is bein' persecuted. So with more great difficulty, he frees his mother by turnin' her persecutors into stone, then returns to his birthplace with his mother and his wife.

"Now the grandfather, rememberin' what the oracle had said long ago, flees when he sees Perseus. But, you see, it is written in the stars. And one day, Perseus is throwin' the discus durin' some athletic games where his grandfather is present, and the discus strikes and kills the ol' man. Perseus is now in line to succeed to his grandfather's throne— which he doesn't want— so he has to go away again and establish his family in another place. Which he does—and this is the family into which the hero Hercules is later born.

"Now, this story is not history, but it reveals a great truth. The hero, Perseus, is forced to leave his familiar world and venture into the unknown. It takes him into strange worlds where he encounters many difficulties. In the process of overcomin' the difficulties he becomes a man. If he did not leave home and take the journey, he would not grow into responsible manhood. So the important thing is the journey, not the destination."

This is not what the girl wants to hear; the only thing on her mind is the destination.

"It's the hero's journey," the harbour pilot continues, "and it appears again and again in mythology.

"There's Homer's *Odyssey*, written in Greek in the 6th century BCE. The hero, Odysseus, is detained on an island under the rule of the sea-nymph Calypso—which means 'concealer'. The god Zeus persuades Calypso to let him go. Odysseus makes his escape on a raft which Zeus tells him how to construct, then spends a long and perilous time at sea before he eventually arrives, unconscious, to the place of his birth.

"There's Virgil's *Aeneid*, written in Latin, in the 1st century CE. Here we meet the hero Aeneis in the burnin' ruins of Troy, prepared to fight to his death. But a dream tells him to flee the battle and to found a new Troy in a distant land across the sea. Carryin' his household gods, Aeneis escapes from the ruins, and there follows seven long years of treacherous wanderin'. Finally, Aeneis arrives in Italy and founds the glorious city of Rome."

"Enough of ancient mythology," thinks the girl. But the harbour pilot goes on.

"And then there's Dante's *Divine Comedy*, written in Italian in the 13th century where we first meet Pilgrim in Inferno—which is hell. Led by the lady Beatrice—which means 'beloved'—he finds the way out of his imprisonment

43

is through the spiritual and civil renewal of the whole of humanity. This leads him to Purgatorio—which is purgatory—where he must spend a long time strugglin' toward the light so that his spirit can be purified in order to be worthy to ascend into heaven. By the end of this struggle, Pilgrim advances to Paradiso—heaven—that is an earthly state of natural perfection.

"Now, no matter what the language or the period or the culture, the story is always the same. The hero finds himself in some kind of situation from which he must escape. It involves leavin' his familiar world behind and embarkin' on a long and perilous journey. He must undertake the adventure alone—but he is not without aid. For once he commits to the mission, the gods assist him along the way. Then after endurin' many difficult trials, he eventually reaches his goal.

"The interestin' thing about this is that the hero is a very ordinary person who discovers along the way that he can do extraordinary things. Maybe the purpose is to tell us we were born for somethin' different from what we are doin'. The idea bein' that the story will point us in the right direction. You see, your father followed the path of the hero's journey. And for him the journey was to follow the route of the Vikings to the New World.

"Think back now about 40,000 years ago when the present human species emerged from earlier hominids.

Humans were land-borne and the sea was a mystery. Then someone discovered that you could float on a log and use your hands for paddles. Then they discovered you could tie logs together and use wood in place of hands. This led to the first rowboat. And then to galleys with oars and then to sailin' ships which led to the crossin' of oceans and the exploration of whole new worlds.

"Now look at the Viking contribution in all this. Back in the 4th and 3rd centuries BCE, they already have highly crafted ships which use 20 oarsmen. Then, about the year 800, their ships have thirty oars and a light mast with a square sail. A hundred years later, the ships are sturdy enough to sail the ocean with 32 oars and strong square sails.

"You see, long sea voyages were rare before the 16th century. Yet as far back as the 10th century, Nordic seafarers crossed the North Atlantic and sailed along the coast of North America. How far south they reached is in dispute, but your father proved they could have made it all the way to Massachusetts. He was certain he had reached Vinland although he will probably never be credited with its discovery. But the Vikings were likewise never properly credited with the discovery of America.

"Why? Because people will accept information only if it fits into their existin' worldview. The ancient Viking knowledge about American lands had to be interpreted in terms of a mediaeval worldview. And that view held that there were only three continents: Asia, Africa and Europe. You see, back then, Europeans believed that Greenland was connected to a land bridge that extended from Norway to northwest Asia. They thought the Atlantic Ocean was practically a land-locked sea.

"Now, the same thing has happened with regard to your father. He followed the clues left by those ancient mariners and it took him to Massachusetts. For him, that was all the proof he needed. But the prevailin' scientific worldview required material evidence. He didn't have a runestone to prove it—but that doesn't mean he didn't reach his goal. Remember: it's the journey, not the destination.

"So, you see," the harbour pilot concludes, as he sips the last of his nightly glass of rum, "Vinland remains an unsolved mystery because people are forgettin' one simple thing."

"And what is that one simple thing?" she asks.

"Ah, that," he replies, "I will tell you—"

"I know, I know," she interrupts, "you will tell me tomorrow."

COMMENTARY ON NARRATIVE III

PATH OF THE HERO'S JOURNEY

1. The Ordinary World
2. The Call to Adventure
3. Meeting of the Mentor
4. Refusal of the Call

Now it is time to . . .

5. CROSS THE FIRST THRESHOLD

The heroine must commit to the adventure and fully enter the Special World. She must agree to face the consequences of dealing with the problem or challenge. Our heroine begins to listen, forced to re-think her mission. It is a psychological danger, a movement from changing the world to changing her mind about the world. It leads to . . .

6. TESTS, ALLIES AND ENEMIES.

Our heroine will encounter new challenges once over the threshold as she begins to learn the rules of the Special World. We watch her react under stress. Put succinctly, the quest itself is now in question. As a result, our heroine's mindset is turned upside down, challenged by the stories the harbour pilot has shared with her.

Narrative IV
Out of the Sea Mist
The Mystery of Vinland Revealed

Imagine if you will, the beautiful *Splendour of the Seas* streaming southward in the waters of the North Atlantic Ocean, heading toward the island of Newfoundland. The Canadian pilot will leave the ship at the next port of call, once he guides the vessel safely in and out of St. John's rocky harbour. Tonight will be the final conversation between the old seaman and the young Norwegian girl.

"You see," the harbour pilot begins, as he tosses back another healthy—or not so healthy—glass of rum, "the quest is not *where* Vinland exists; it's *how* it exists. What it represents. You will not find your Vinland by searchin' for it only as a sign because, for you, Vinland is more than a sign. It's a symbol."

"What's the difference?" the girl wants to know.

"A sign," he replies, "is a mark or a shape that refers to somethin', and it is always less than what it represents. Like those twenty-four letters of the ol' Norse runic alphabet. At one level, they are just signs.

"Now a symbol, by contrast, represents somethin' else, and it always stands for more than its obvious or immediate meaning. Like your L-runestone which is also a symbol for

51

water. It's like a code for somethin' that cannot be expressed in words alone.

"Now, when a symbol is explored, it can lead to ideas that go beyond reason and even logic. Take the sea mist, for example. As a sign, it refers to a weather condition. But as a symbol, it can mean a number of things: like limited vision, faulty understandin', or a need to clear the air mentally or emotionally."

"So what you're saying is . . ." the girl prods.

"What I'm sayin' is that your Vinland will be revealed once you get clear on your quest. You see, it doesn't matter if the Viking sagas tell conflictin' or illogical stories. Because it may well be that they are not intended to be read only as historical signs but also as mythological symbols. Maybe what they are sayin' is that Vinland is the fabled quest, like the search for the Holy Grail or the fountain of youth. The point is to make the quest."

"But what about the wild grapes and sweet-tasting dew?" she asks.

"Do you remember", he says, "my tellin' you about the great mythic journeys? About the *Odyssey*, the *Aeneid* and the *Divine Comedy*?"

"Yes," she replies.

"Well, now I'm goin' to tell you another one. And this one is like your quest for Vinland because it's a journey that some take to be story and others take to be history. It's a story and/or history of a nomadic people in the Middle East—the Habiru or Hebrew tribes—originatin' in Canaan but migratin', accordin' to conditions, to places in and around the ancient civilizations of Babylon and Sumer. Now accordin' to the story or history, there was a severe drought in Canaan so twelve of these tribes move south to the land of Goshen which is Egypt. They stay for a lengthy time there and become known as 'the children of Israel livin' in the land of Egypt'.

"One version of the story suggests that, for a period of 150 years, there are Semitic rulers known as Hyksos in Egypt who would, of course, be friendly to these migratin' tribes. Another version—and the more popular one—suggests that a young man from one of these tribes whose name was Joseph is sold into Egypt by his brothers, and because he has the extraordinary gift of interpretin' dreams, earns favour with the Egyptian Pharaoh and, as a result, paves the way for his relatives, the children of Israel, to live and thrive in this land of plenty durin' the drought in Canaan.

"Let's stay with the second version.

"Now, accordin' to the first chapter of Exodus, there arose a new king in Egypt, who knew not Joseph. And he said unto his people: 'Behold, the people of the children of Israel are too many and too mighty for us; come, let us deal wisely with them lest they multiply and it come to pass that if a war befalls us, they will take the side of our enemy.'

"And you know what happens. The Egyptians make their lives very difficult, forcin' them into slave labour to build great store-cities for the Pharaohs. But as the story unfolds, Moses, raised as an Egyptian prince, discovers his Hebrew heritage and determines to free these Israelites and lead them home. Through the divine intervention of their god Yahweh, they escape from bondage by crossin' the Red Sea. This event is followed by forty years of wanderin' in the wilderness, after which time they arrive in Palestine, the 'land of milk and honey'.

"Now, the first thing that is obvious is this is another version of the Hero's Journey. Imprisonment, escape, wilderness, arrival. The same pattern that we see over and over again. No matter if it is story or history, it is teachin' a mighty lesson. But there's more. Because we can hardly say that after that long forty years of wanderin' in the wilderness—much longer than it should take by about thirty-nine and a half years, by the way—we can hardly say they arrived in a land flowin' with milk and honey. Palestine was a desert!

"Now, supposin' today we don't know where this place Palestine or Israel is, and we set out lookin' for it. If we have our mind set on findin' a land flowin' with milk and honey, we will be sorely led off track. You see, milk and honey are not *signs* that point to a particular physical location. Rather, they are *symbols* and, as such, refer to somethin' much deeper and much more meaningful."

"How do you mean?" the girl asks.

"Well—and this is very interestin'—the thing about milk and honey is that they are both natural but transformed substances. The cow eats grass from the field and turns it into milk. The bee takes nectar from the flower and turns it into honey. Milk and honey are still natural substances, but they have been transformed in the process. So the story is pointin' to a greater mystery, that we should be transformed ourselves. And we do this, like in the hero's journey, by escapin' from our psychological or social imprisonment, and goin' into the wilderness, that dark night of the soul where we grow up. And then, after a long and sometimes painful process, we arrive at a new level of awareness. You see, once again, a symbol is greater than a sign and a story is greater than a history."

"But how does that apply to Vinland?" the girl wants to know.

"Well, think about the idea of sweet-tastin' dew and grape vines," he says.

"What about them?"

"Well, where does dew come from?"

"From the air, I guess," she says.

"That's right, but how does air turn into dew?"

"I don't know," she replies.

"Well, when air is cooled to its saturation point, water condenses on blades of grass and other objects that are not in extensive contact with the earth. In other words, dew comes from a natural substance that has been transformed."

"Right," the girl muses out loud.

"And what naturally happens to grapes?" he asks.

"Well, they ferment and turn into wine. Natural but transformed...." she muses.

"You see", he continues, "maybe the writers of the sagas were usin' these symbols to express their sense of wonder and achievement. Maybe they were sayin' they found their Vinland by leavin' the ordinary world and venturin' into the unknown."

"So the runestones don't matter?" she questions.

"*Au contraire,*" he responds. "Maybe we need to look for their deeper meanin' as well."

"Like how?" she wants to know.

The old seaman points to the runestone pendant the Norwegian girl wears around her neck. "I notice you always wear that," he says, "Why?"

"Well, it's a kind of good luck charm."

"In what way?" he probes.

"I don't know. I've never thought about it," she says.

"Well, it's the symbol for water. Maybe your Vinland is somehow connected to water," he suggests.

"Well, that's true. I am following my father's sea voyage", she responds.

"No, I'm thinkin' somethin' different from that," he replies. "Otherwise, your father would have had the same runestone, don't you think? His was the Sowulo, the S-rune, the rune for seafarers."

"Well, I don't know how it's connected, then," she says.

The harbour pilot looks at her. "Tell me," he says, "what did you want to do before you set out on your father's journey?"

"I don't remember," she replies.

"Well, think about it now. If you could do anything you want to do, what would it be? What is the thing that interests you more than anything else?"

"Well, I'd like to help people stay young and healthy," she says.

"You see, there you go!"

"But I'm not trained to do that kind of work," she says.

"Well, now," he replies, "I am goin' to tell you a strange and unexplainable truth. When you dare to follow your quest—the thing that most interests you in life—four things happen. First, you will find yourself doin' somethin' you were not trained to do. Second, everythin' you need will be provided. Third, you will lead a very adventurous life. And finally, you will be free from all the traditional obligations that characterize life for the majority of people on the planet."

"But what about my father?" she says. "About their laughing at him?"

"You want to help people stay young and healthy?"

"Yes, but—"

"Well, so do I. So I give 'em somethin' to laugh about. Do you know there was a man named Norman Cousins, a writer of some kind, who discovered that people could laugh themselves to health? You know how he found out? Well, he was diagnosed with a degenerative disease and wasn't given much of a chance. But he was determined to beat it and was smart enough to realize that our state of mind has a lot to do with our state of health. So he started readin' jokes and watchin' comedies. And guess what? He got better! Then he started helpin' other people get better usin' laughter as the medicine."

"But it's different when they're laughing *at* you."

"*Au contraire* again. Newfoundlanders are the butt of jokes all the time. Some of them are very funny."

"How can you say that when they're making fun of you?"

"Well, take this one, for example. There was this ol' Newfie man who died and wanted to be buried at sea. Know what happened?"

"No, what?"

"Six men drowned diggin' his grave."

"Oh, my goodness," she says.

"That's funny!" he says. "Don't you find that funny?"

The girl does not respond.

"You don't laugh very much, do you?" he says. "In fact, you don't laugh at all."

There is silence. Then the harbor pilot speaks again.

"Okay, here's another one. Quebec Hydro is puttin' up some new power lines and they need a whole lot of new Hydro poles put in, eh. So they hire a Newfie crew along with their Quebec crew to do the job. At the end of the first day, the boss asks the foreman of the Newfie crew how many poles they put in, and the Newfie foreman says 'Two'. 'Only two?' exclaims the boss. 'My Quebec crew put in 18!' The Newfie looks the boss straight in the eyes, 'Yeah, boy,' he says, 'but did you see how far they left 'em stickin' out of the ground!'"

The girl looks at him curiously. She shows no emotion.

"Okay, how about this one," the harbour pilot tries again. "These two Newfies rent a dory—that's a little boat with two oars, you know—to go out fishin'. They drop their fishin' lines in one spot and don't even get a nibble. They row a bit further and try again, still no fish. Then they get to this third spot, and lo and behold, the fish are bitin' like crazy and they're pullin' 'em in, one right after the other.

"One Newfie turns to the other, 'Hey, Joe,' he says, 'Me thinks we should mark this spot.' The second Newfie says, 'Yeah, boy, me thinks you's right.' and he takes a big piece of chalk out of 'is pocket, leans over and marks a big 'X' on the side of the boat. The first Newfie looks straight at 'im and says, 'You know, Joe, you's really stupid. You think now they's gonna rent us the same boat ag'in tomorrow?'"

The girl looks straight at him, expressionless.

"You see, laughter is great medicine," he says.

"But don't you feel hurt or angry or upset when people make fun of you like that?" she asks.

"Not at all. Because we know the origin," he replies. "You see, we were the last of ten provinces to join the dominion of Canada. It only happened in 1949. Before that, we were an isolated island out in the north Atlantic and pretty much left to fend for ourselves. We didn't have the communication links and amenities that the other nine provinces enjoyed, eh. And bein' an island, we didn't have access to most of their goods and services.

"Now it's the early 1950's and they do some standard IQ testin' of children right across the country, includin', for the first time, this new province of Newfoundland. There are a whole lot of questions on the test comparin' things with oranges in shape and size. And our children got those questions wrong because up to that time there had never been any oranges imported into Newfoundland. It was the first IQ testin' in the province and because the scores were lower compared to the rest of Canada, they get this idea in their heads that Newfoundlanders are two bricks short of a load and have been thinkin' that way about us ever since."

"Oh, that's awful," the girl says.

"Well, maybe, but like I say, we know better so we laugh with 'em. We can handle it. What's awful is that half a century has gone by and they are still misinterpretin' intelligence tests in Canada.

"But it's not Newfoundland this time. It's the native children in northern Canada. Intelligence testin' doesn't reflect their culture or their situation."

"So," she queries, "they think native children are, what is that you say, two bricks . . .?"

"Short of a load," he repeats. "You know, slow. One time they send this psychologist up there to find out why these native children keep failin' the tests. And he takes this one native boy outside for a walk and asks him some logic questions, like 'Why do you wear seat belts when you are ridin' in a car?' and the native boy answers, 'So the cops won't stop you.' Well, that isn't the right answer, so the kid gets a zero. Then the psychologist goes to the next question. 'Why do you put license plates on your car?' he asks, and the kid gives him the same answer, 'So the cops won't stop you.' Wrong answer again, another zero. So then the psychologist decides to switch gears and ask a question that isn't about motor vehicles; he says, 'When you are home at night, why do you turn off the lights in the rooms you are not usin'?' and the boy answers, 'So the cops won't know you're home.' Wrong answer, another zero. Then the psychologist realizes that this kid isn't stupid. In fact, he is street smart because it is obvious that these native people are bein' harassed by the police.

"Now all this time the two of 'em have been walkin' in the woods and the psychologist realizes that he is lost. He asks the boy, 'Which way is west?' and the kid doesn't know. Then the psychologist says, 'Well, we're lost and I don't know how to get back.' An' the boy says, 'Oh, that's easy. We just go over there to that tree, then turn right and walk over to that other tree an' . . .

"Get what I'm sayin'? The kid was smart, alright. He knew what he had to know to survive up there in that harsh environment. Well, the psychologist put in his report and said, 'Maybe the boy failed the questions on the intelligence test, but, let me tell you, if I'm ever lost in the forest, I want to be with him!'

"So, you see, there is an important lesson in all this. First, we must be independent of the good opinion of others. Second, we must detach ourselves from the outcome. Third, we must have no investment in power over other people."

"So it doesn't matter what they think about my father?" she says.

"That's right," he replies, "And it doesn't matter what they think about you.

"Remember this: you are the pilot of your own life. You have got to set your own coordinates and follow your own course. It won't always take you into an open sea. And sometimes the channels will be narrow. You've got to know your depth and watch out for the rocks. But stay the course and it will take you to your Vinland."

And with that he finishes off the last of his bottle of rum . . . and bids the Norwegian girl good-bye.

COMMENTARY ON NARRATIVE IV

PATH OF THE HERO'S JOURNEY
1. The Ordinary World
2. The Call to Adventure
3. Meeting of the Mentor
4. Refusal of the Call
5. Crossing the First Threshold
6. Tests, Allies and Enemies
And now we come to . . .

7. APPROACH TO THE INNERMOST CAVE

The heroine comes at last to the place where the object of the quest is hidden. What is the object of the quest? Not to change the world—but to change her mind about the world. Put another way, the heroine sets out on a *mission* but discovers, in the process, that she is to achieve *submission*. That is the more difficult task. For submission to what? That is what the heroine must now figure out. And it leads to . . .

8. THE SUPREME ORDEAL

Here the heroine faces her greatest challenge, not knowing if she will succeed or fail. Once again, it is not a physical jeopardy but a moral one. "You are the pilot of your own life," the mentor has told her. "You have to set your own coordinates and follow your own course." It is at this point the harbor pilot bids the girl farewell. Now the heroine is on her own.

Before leaving, however, the harbor pilot has revealed a further bit of wisdom: the important connection between story and history. This is the point where story and history converge, where the physical and the metaphysical speak the same language. Here we realize the power of the archetypal images. They are universal and they have the power to heal. They call us to adventure, to embark on the journey. And the journey itself will teach that *story* creates *history*. That is to say, what we believe, what we tell ourselves, determines, to a great extent, what happens to us. We are creating our future with what we are thinking now.

Notice that every Narrative begins with the words "Imagine if you will...". Imagining connects us to the subconscious mind. William James once stated that the power to move the world is in the subconscious mind. While the conscious mind is aware of everyday secondary experience, the subconscious mind is connected with the entire system. In short, events are affected by what we imagine.

Narrative V

Water, Water Everywhere

An Old Secret for a New World

Imagine if you will, the *Splendour of the Seas* pulling away from St John's harbour, heading for the great continental landmass of North America. The harbour pilot stands alongside the captain on the ship's bridge, guiding the great vessel through the rocky channel toward the open sea. When the ship has progressed safely outside the harbour limits, the Newfoundlander bids the captain farewell and steps aboard the small pilot vessel broadside, which returns him to his native shore.

Night falls. The Norwegian girl makes her way to the Viking Crown Lounge for her usual evening shift. But tonight, it will be different. The old seaman will no longer be there. With an air of melancholy, she prepares to once again serve the beer, the wine and the cocktails to those late night "party animals". She enters the lounge and stares blankly through the long windows into the black starlit sky. Out to Polaris and Ursa Major and Cassiopeia and Andromeda. Ah, she muses, such a simple and unschooled man, he was, yet such a complex and wise human being....

She walks over to the chair her old friend occupied every evening during the long ocean crossing. Now that he is home in Newfoundland, she wonders, is he finally enjoying a drink of his customary screech. She glances at the small bar table where each night she would set down his 'bo'ole' of rum.

But what is this? There, sitting on the table? The empty bottle, with the cork intact, and a sheet of notepaper wrapped around it, tied with a string. On the outside of the paper, scribbled in pencil is written...

To the Norwegian girl,
who brings an old secret
to a new world.

Old secret? What old secret? Oh yes, that's right. The very first night they met, she had made mention of an old Scandinavian secret.

She unties the string and reads the message. "Soon you will arrive in a land," it says, "where men and women search relentlessly for ways to ward off disease and old age. Never has the quest to look and feel younger been more pursued than at the present time. North Americans try diets, drugs, hormones, face-lifts, face peels, masks, herbs, cellular injections, even cosmetic surgery to postpone what they fear to be the inevitable.

"More serious than this, despite an annual health care expenditure estimated to reach $1.6 trillion by the year 2000, Americans suffer ever-increasing complaints from gastritis, duodenitis, heartburn, colitis, false appendicitis, hiatus hernia, rheumatoid arthritis, lower back pain, angina, headaches, stress and depression, high blood pressure, hypertension, high cholesterol, excess body weight, asthma and allergies.

"You will remember," it goes on, "that, in the Icelandic sagas, while much is said of fate, the characters seem to control their own destinies. You may believe you were *fated* to *search for* the runestone that will put an end to an unsolved mystery. I believe the opposite is true: that you are *destined* to *reveal* the runestone that will put an end to an unsolved mystery. For while there are arguably a number of ingredients involved in staying young and healthy, I believe you hold the key to a very critical one of them, and that your quest is embodied in the very symbol you wear around your neck."

The girl stares at the page. She wears the L- runestone, the symbol for water.

"Water, water everywhere, nor any drop to drink," she finds herself reciting. Her grandmother had oft quoted those lines from "The Rhyme of the Ancient Mariner", referring to the way people failed to understand how essential water is to their well-being. Everyone knows water is good for the body, she would say. But they do not realize what happens if it does not receive its daily requirements.

Water. Yes, her grandmother had always said that the fountain of youth was a water fountain. And when people came to her for healing, she would often say, "You are not sick; you are thirsty!"

Water, the grandmother taught her, was truly a sacred symbol to Scandinavians. Ancient tradition reminded them that life originated in the sea. When, in the course of long evolution, gills turned into lungs and creatures emerged from the sea onto the land, their dependencies on the life-giving properties of water did not change. But something else did. Life on land guaranteed no ready water supply. So, in its wisdom, the brain created a complex water rationing system to keep the organism alive.

Human beings, she said, have inherited this water rationing system. And today, every function of the human body is monitored and pegged to the flow of water, because water management is the only way the body can make sure enough water and the nutrients it carries will first reach the more vital organs. That means the less vital organs—the ones not critical to immediate survival—must take whatever is left or perhaps go without altogether. The human brain must constantly decide which parts will get water at the expense of others, and it gives itself absolute priority over all other systems. The brain comprises only one-fiftieth of the total body weight, but it receives one-fifth of the circulation of the blood.

If the body continually fails to get enough water, cautioned her grandmother, chronic dehydration sets in and some of the less vital functions begin to break down. These conditions are warning signals sent out by the body's water rationing system. But they are not understood as such. Instead, we translate them as conditions of disease and give them various names: gastritis, duodenitis, heartburn, colitis, false appendicitis, hiatus hernia, rheumatoid arthritis, lower back pain, angina, headaches, stress and depression, high blood pressure, hypertension, high cholesterol, excess body weight, asthma and allergies. And then we try to identify a particular substance that might be the cause of the so-called disease. Finally, we treat the condition with drugs instead of curing it with water.

How did this mindset come about? Her grandmother said it came from applying the method we had already developed for the study of chemistry to the study of the human body. Chemistry looks at solid particles because these solids are considered to be the active elements in nature. As in chemistry, medical researchers automatically assumed that the solid matter is what regulates the functions of the body. But the human body is composed of twenty-five percent solid matter and seventy-five percent water. And brain tissue is said to be eighty-five percent water. At least

73

three times as much water as solid matter, yet the water content of the body was assumed to act only as a means of transport.

Based on this assumption of the role of water, she taught her granddaughter, it became the practice to regard "dry mouth" as the pre-eminent sign that the body needs water, and it is further assumed that if this sense of "dry mouth" is not present, then there must be no further need for water. Truth is, "dry mouth" is the last sign the body needs water.

The old Scandinavian secret about the human body that will enable people to stay young and healthy, she concluded, is simply this. It is the *solute*—the water content—not the *solvent*—the solid matter—that regulates the functions of the body, including the activity of the solids that are dissolved in it. Every function of the body is monitored and pegged to the efficient flow of water. When the body is not sufficiently hydrated, a rationing and distribution system for the available water goes into effect according to a predetermined priority program—a form of drought management. This is the only way of making sure that not only an adequate amount of water, but also its transported elements (hormones, chemical messengers and nutrients) first reach the vital organs. This complex water rationing system and distribution process remains in operation until the body receives unmistakable signals that it has gained access to an adequate water supply.

Chronic dehydration: that is the culprit, proclaimed her grandmother. And it is caused by persistent water shortage that has become established over time. Like any other deficiency such as Vitamin C deficiency in scurvy, Vitamin B deficiency in beriberi, iron deficiency in anemia or Vitamin D deficiency in rickets, the obvious means of treatment is to provide the missing ingredient. In the same way, if we can recognize the health implications of chronic dehydration, their prevention, and even cure, becomes very simple.

The solution, her grandmother preached, for both the prevention and treatment of chronic dehydration-produced diseases is water intake on a regular basis. It is the simplest— and in many cases the most effective—form of treatment in medicine. The body needs a minimum of six to eight glasses of pure water a day. The best times to drink water, she taught the girl, are one glass a half hour before taking food— breakfast, lunch and dinner—and a similar amount two and a half hours after each meal. This is the very minimum amount of water the body needs. And just to make sure, two more glasses of water should be taken around the heaviest meal or before going to bed.

The bottom line is this: the same way dehydration will in time produce premature aging and disease, a well-regulated and constantly alert attention to daily water intake will prevent them. The moment people learn this secret and respond to it, the medical practice of treating pain with medications will transform into a thoughtful preventive approach to health care.

The *Splendour of the Seas* streams toward the port of Boston. The girl gazes out the window at the emerging coastline of the New World. She would find her Vinland here, but as the harbour pilot had surmised, it would not be in the form she had expected. Now she realizes she answered her own call to adventure and that she has embarked on her own heroic journey.

Who really was this harbour pilot, she muses. Could theirs have been but a chance encounter? For he had shown her through those great mythic stories that, when a heroine commits to a mission, she receives help along the way. Was he perhaps sent to guide her through the Viking Runes and Viking Sagas, to tell her about the Ancient Rhymes and the Ancient Mariners?

And what of her father, who had retraced the route of those ancient mariners in a small, open ship. Had he perhaps sailed on ahead to bring her to these shores?

The girl leaves the Viking Crown Lounge and walks to an outside deck. Holding the empty bottle and with pen in hand, she scribbles a note on the back of the harbour pilot's message.

Dear Mother,

I have found Vinland—exactly where father said it was. And here is the runestone to prove it. Once its message has been translated on these shores, I shall return home.

The Norwegian girl removes the runestone from her neck, tucks it with the note inside the empty bottle, and fastens the cork. Then she reaches out and tosses the 'bo'ole' into the vast Atlantic Ocean.

"Ah, the splendour of the sea!" she muses. And then she bursts out laughing.

COMMENTARY ON NARRATIVE V

PATH OF THE HEROINE'S JOURNEY

1. The Ordinary World
2. The Call to Adventure
3. Meeting of the Mentor
4. Refusal of the Call
5. Crossing the First Threshold
6. Tests, Allies and Enemies
7. Approach to the Innermost Cave
8. The Supreme Ordeal

Now it is time to . . .

9. SEIZE THE SWORD AND TAKE THE REWARD

Our heroine now takes possession of the treasure, the reward. In this case, it is knowledge and experience that leads to reconciliation. And the final steps . . .

10. THE ROAD BACK

The heroine must deal with the consequences of confronting her demons, and reconcile with those she has thwarted, misjudged or mistreated. And then the . . .

11. RESURRECTION

The heroine, who has now been in the Special World, must use that experience to fulfill her mission before returning to the ordinary world. It is a kind of final test, to see if she has truly learned her lesson. She must then make preparation to return to the ordinary world, to . . .

12 RETURN WITH THE ELIXIR

Our heroine, once back in the ordinary world, has the treasure, the lesson from the Special World. It is the magic potion with the power to heal.

THE HEROINE'S JOURNEY
A Summary

1. THE ORDINARY WORLD

If our heroine were to choose to stay in the Ordinary World, she must settle for the beliefs and rituals of the culture into which she is born.

2. THE CALL TO ADVENTURE

The Ordinary World is the Imprisonment; the Call to Adventure is the Escape. From thereon it's Wilderness until Arrival at stage 12. The Wilderness is where the inner work gets done.

3. MEETING OF THE MENTOR

If the heroine answers the Call to Adventure, if she sets out on a mission, the Universe will conspire to help her. Meeting of the Mentor is the first sign the Universe is on side.

4. REFUSAL OF THE CALL

Now we come to the first roadblock and encounter a critical element in the Heroine's Journey: our heroine sets out on a *mission* but discovers, in the process, that she is to achieve *submission*. Is she willing to submit? And, if so, submit to what? That is the riddle the heroine must solve.

5.   CROSSING THE FIRST THRESHOLD

The Heroine must retreat from the ordinary world to those causal zones of the psyche where the difficulties really lie. She cannot solve the riddle by returning to the good old days. Rather she must clarify the difficulties and get rid of them.

6.   TESTS, ALLIES AND ENEMIES

The idea at this juncture is that everything we experience, positive and negative, is grist for the mill. It is put there for our learning, to help us achieve the goal. That is the essence of the adventure.

7.   APPROACH TO THE INNERMOST CAVE

The passage of the mythical Hero(ine) may be over water, but fundamentally, it is inward—into depths where obscure resistances are overcome, and long-lost forgotten powers are revisited, to be made available for the transfiguration of the world.

8.   THE SUPREME ORDEAL

The Hero(ine)'s perilous journey is not so much one of discovery but of rediscovery. The godly powers sought and dangerously won are revealed to have been within the heart of the heroine the whole time.

9.   REWARD (SEIZING THE SWORD)

The point is, that before such and such can be done on earth, this other, more important primary thing has to be brought to pass within the labyrinth of our minds. We have not to risk the adventure alone for the heroes of all time have gone before us; the labyrinth is thoroughly known. We have only to follow the path.

10.   THE ROAD BACK

This stage represents a checkpoint, as it were. Have you really learned the lesson? Can you walk the talk? Is what you do equal to what you say?

11.   RESURRECTION

The Heroine has died as an ordinary person and is resurrected as an eternal being; i.e., she has been reborn. Her second solemn task and deed is to return to us transfigured and to teach the lesson she has learned of life renewed.

12.   RETURN WITH THE ELIXIR

The elixir is the transfigured self. The Hero(ine) is a symbol of the divine creative and redemptive image that is hidden within us all, only waiting to be known and rendered into life.

ACKNOWLEDGEMENTS

Anyone familiar with the outstanding scholarship of anthropologist Joseph Campbell will immediately recognize my indebtedness to him. Indeed, it was because of his writings about the mythological Hero's Journey that I felt inspired to create, first, a modern Mayan Hero myth for the benefit of travelers who journey from the New World to the Old, and now, a companion Heroine myth based on Viking origins for travelers journeying from the Old World to the New.

I also wish to acknowledge here the pioneering work of Dr. F. Batmanghelidj on the natural healing power of water. Those familiar with his work and writings will recognize my indebtedness to him as well. For those interested in further exploring the subject, I recommend his book "Your Body's Many Cries for Water", first published in 1992.

For an instructive and well-presented understanding of Viking Runes, I recommend the beautiful small book entitled RUNES by Catherine and Orla Duane, first published in 1997. There you will find verses and interpretations for each of the 24 Runic symbols of the Common Futhark.

Thank you to my editor Ken Johnson for help and support along the way. Ken has been my right-hand man on this and numerous creative projects. I also acknowledge the people at Trafford Publishing who have guided me through the publication process for this and previous books.

And a very special thanks to Royal Caribbean Cruise Lines for inviting me to lecture on their beautiful cruise ship, *Splendour of the Seas*, on a transatlantic crossing from London to Boston. Thank you also to all those cruise passengers for their abiding interest in the power of myth as we travelled together from the Old World to the New.

ABOUT THE AUTHOR

Pamela J Peck is an author, lecturer, composer and playwright whose professional interest is education for a global perspective, and the application of social science knowledge to the practical concerns of everyday life. Canadian born, she holds the degrees of Bachelor of Arts in Psychology and Religion (Mount Allison University), Bachelor of Social Work, Master of Social Work and PhD in Anthropology (UBC). She was a Research Associate at the University of Delhi in India and a Research Fellow at the University of the South Pacific in Fiji.

Pamela has traveled to more than one hundred countries around the world and has lived and studied in many of them. She uses her cultural experiences to infuse and inform her novels, short stories, screenplays and stage musicals. Drawing on the archetypal structure of classical mythology and Jungian psychology, her creative works embody timeless and universal principles. Her stories appeal to people of all ages as she takes us on magical and adventurous journeys to the far corners of the outer world, and into the inner recesses of the human mind.

Printed in the United States
By Bookmasters